All puppies dream about Christmas.

One little white dog gets especially
carried away. His name is Tucker.

After the first big snowstorm,
Tucker makes a snowman for Santa.

But when Tucker gets hungry, he eats the carrot nose!

Tucker sniffs all the Christmas trees
until he finds just the right one.

He loves getting into all the boxes of decorations...

but he has a hard time getting back out again.

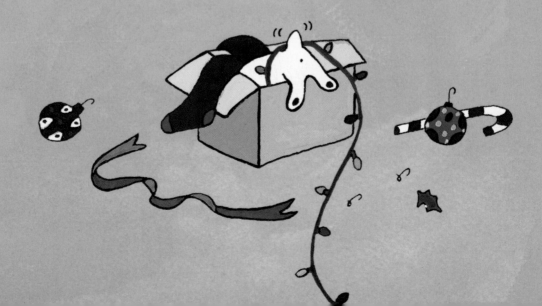

That Tucker! He's cuter than an elf and just as busy.

With all the mistletoeing...

"BARK THE HERALD ANGELS SING!"

and the Christmas caroling...

and the holiday baking—
Oh, no!

LOOK OUT, TUCKER!

That pan was HOT!

Tucker's burned his nose.

Ouch, Tucker!

Now Tucker's nose is very red, and he's exhausted.

Good thing it's time for him to hang his stocking and go to bed.

Good night, Tucker!
May visions of dog
biscuits dance in
your head.

JINGLE
JINGLE

While Tucker is sleeping, guess
who flies by his window?

That's right. It's Santa!

"Ho, ho, ho, Tucker!" shouts Santa.
"Look at your bright red nose! Come along with
me — I want you in front with my reindeer."

Tucker's really carried away now.
Good boy, Tucker!

All night long, Tucker and Santa
go up and down chimneys.

They stop at every house for milk and cookies.

Tucker always remembers to bring some carrots back up to the reindeer.

By sunrise, Tucker is tuckered out. Santa
knows his little helper needs to go home.

DEAR TUCKER, THANK YOU FOR ALL YOUR HELP! I HOPE THESE ANTLERS FIT. HUGE LOVE, SANTA XO

Santa drops Tucker off at his house, along with a very special present.

Merry Christmas, Tucker!

Finally it's time for Tucker to get some sleep